Where is Simone?

May I have your attention, please, was announced. *Will Simone Green please report to the information desk on the main level. Thank you.*

"That announcement is no good," Cam said. "Simone won't understand it. It should have been made in French."

Mr. Jansen returned the pen and forms to the airline's desk. Then Cam, her parents, Eric, and Aunt Molly began to walk toward the exit.

"Wait," Aunt Molly said. "I forgot something."

"What now?" Mrs. Jansen asked as Aunt Molly ran back to the bench.

A moment later Aunt Molly returned carrying Eric's bag of popcorn. She took some from the bag and ate it as she walked.

"Wait," Eric said.

"Not again," Mrs. Jansen told him. "We have to get home."

"But I know where to find Simone."

The Cam Jansen Adventure Series

DON'T FORGET ABOUT THE YOUNG CAM JANSEN
SERIES FOR YOUNGER READERS!

CamJansen
The Mystery of Flight 54

David A. Adler
Illustrated by Susanna Natti

PUFFIN BOOKS
Published by Penguin Group
Penguin Young Readers Group,
345 Hudson Street, New York, New York 10014, U.S.A.
Penguin Books Ltd, 80 Strand, London WC2R ORL, England
Penguin Books Australia Ltd, 250 Camberwell Road, Camberwell, Victoria 3124, Australia
Penguin Books Canada Ltd, 10 Alcorn Avenue, Toronto, Ontario, Canada M4V 3B2
Penguin Books (N.Z.) Ltd, 182-190 Wairau Road, Auckland 10, New Zealand

First published in the United States of America by Viking,
a division of Penguin Books USA Inc., 1989
Published by Puffin Books, 1992
Reissued, 1999, 2004

3 5 7 9 10 8 6 4

THE LIBRARY OF CONGRESS HAS CATALOGED THE 1992 PUFFIN EDITION AS FOLLOWS:
Adler, David A.
Cam Jansen and the mystery of flight 54 / by David A. Adler;
Illustrated by Susanna Natti.
p. cm.—(A Cam Jansen adventure; 12)
Summary: Fifth-grade sleuth Cam Jansen and her friend Eric combine wits
to solve the disappearance of a young French girl.
ISBN 0-14-036104-9
[1. Mystery and detective stories.] I. Natti, Susanna, ill. II. Title.
III. Series: Adler, David A. Cam Jansen adventure; 12.
[PZ7.A2615Caak 1992] [Fic]—dc20 92-5329

This edition ISBN 0-14-240179-X

Printed in the United States of America

RL: 2.3

**To Renée
with love**

Chapter One

"I should have stayed home," Mrs. Jansen said. She was sitting next to Mr. Jansen on the front seat of their car. Their daughter Cam and her friend Eric Shelton were sitting on the back seat. They were all on their way to the airport to pick up Cam's aunt Molly.

Mrs. Jansen was tapping her fingers on the armrest. "We're having a birthday party in two hours. I should be home to get everything ready."

"Everything *is* ready," Mr. Jansen told her.

"And my parents are there," Eric said. "They know what to do."

Mrs. Jansen was still tapping on the arm-rest. She turned and told Cam and Eric, "Don't let Aunt Molly know about the party. We want her to be surprised."

Mrs. Jansen looked at her watch. "What time is her flight coming in?"

"At 2:00," Mr. Jansen said.

Eric said, "I thought it was due in at 1:54."

Cam closed her eyes and said "*Click*." She always says "*Click*" when she wants to re-member something. Cam says it's the sound her "mental camera" makes when it takes a picture.

"I'm looking at the airline schedule," Cam said with her eyes still closed. "Molly's flight is number 54. It's due in at 1:20."

"I'm sorry," her father said, "but this time

2

HARBORSIDE
NEXT EXIT

your memory is wrong. I'm sure the flight is due in at 2:00."

Cam shook her head. "No, 2 is the gate number."

Cam's mental camera is her memory. She can take one look at something and remember it perfectly. "It's easy for me," Cam often explains. "I have a photograph of everything I see stored in my brain. When I want to remember something, I just look at the photograph."

When Cam was younger, her mother read books about how people remember. She learned that scientists call someone like Cam "eidetic." But most people just say that Cam has a photographic memory.

Cam's real name is Jennifer. But when people found out about her photographic memory and heard her say *"Click,"* they started calling her "The Camera." Soon "The Camera" was shortened to "Cam."

Mrs. Jansen looked at her watch again. "We're late," she said as she tapped her fingers on her handbag. "We'll miss Molly. She'll take a bus to our house and see the cake and the surprise will be ruined."

"Don't worry," Mr. Jansen said as he drove into the airport parking lot. "After Molly gets off the plane, she has to get her luggage. We won't miss her."

Mr. Jansen parked the car. Cam, her parents, and Eric walked into the airport arrivals building. Right inside was a television

screen. On it were numbers that kept changing. Cam looked at the screen.

"Flight 54 is already in."

"We missed her," Mrs. Jansen said. "We missed Molly. She's probably on her way to our house right now."

Chapter Two

"Maybe not," Cam said to her mother. "Maybe Aunt Molly is still waiting for her luggage."

Cam, her parents, and Eric looked quickly at the signs nearby. "It's this way," Cam said. She pointed to her left.

May I have your attention, please, was announced. *The city bus will be leaving in three minutes. Thank you.*

As Cam, her parents, and Eric began to walk to their left, people rushed toward them.

"Hurry, Martha, hurry or we'll miss the bus," a man told the woman next to him. She was carrying a large suitcase which she could hardly lift.

"Look, look, a bear," a small girl said. She pointed to a young man carrying a suitcase and a large toy bear with a pink ribbon wrapped around it.

"We'll look when we get on the bus," the girl's mother said.

Cam, her parents, and Eric moved to the side to let the people rush past. As they moved, a fat older man with a beard bumped into Eric. The man's hat fell off.

"I'm terribly sorry," the man said as he picked up his hat. Then he rushed to the door.

"We have to hurry, too," Mrs. Jansen said, "or we'll miss Molly."

Cam and Eric followed Cam's parents. They turned to the left, walked for a while, and then followed a sign to their right. Mr.

Jansen looked around. There were no more signs and no luggage.

"I think we're lost," Cam whispered to Eric.

They were near a large newspaper, magazine, and snack stand.

"I'm hungry," Eric said. He bought a large bag of popcorn. "Do you want some?" he asked Cam as he opened the bag.

"Don't eat so much," Mrs. Jansen told Eric. "I made sandwiches, salads, and a big cake for the party."

Mr. Jansen asked the woman at the newspaper stand, "Do you know where we can find the luggage from Flight 54?"

"It's that way," she told him and pointed to the right.

Will Doris Johnson please report to the information desk on the main level. Thank you, was announced.

Cam, Cam's parents, and Eric walked to the right. Eric saw a woman standing in the middle of three suitcases. "Look, there's Molly," Mr. Jansen said. He ran to her.

"Oh, Jack," the woman said as she ran to meet Mr. Jansen.

They hugged. When Mrs. Jansen reached them, she hugged Aunt Molly, too.

"And look at you, Jennifer," Aunt Molly said when she saw Cam. "You're so pretty. I love your red hair. And Eric, you look real handsome."

Cam, her parents, and Eric looked at Aunt Molly. She looked at them and smiled. Then Aunt Molly sighed. She sat on one of the suitcases. She put her hands on her knees and said, "I've seen so many interesting places on this trip. I visited Basel and Bristol. No, I think it was Barcelona and Brussels. No, it was Bristol, Bern, and Bologna? Oh I don't know. I get all those 'B' places confused. I'll tell you all about it later. But right now I have to rest. I'm so tired."

Aunt Molly unbuttoned her sweater. Then she saw Eric's bag of popcorn. "Can I have some?" she asked.

"Sure," Eric said.

Will Doris Johnson please report to the information desk. Will Captain Baker please report to Gate 7. Thank you, was announced.

A man wearing a dark blue uniform and captain's hat walked quickly toward them. "First they tell me Gate 2. Now it's Gate 7," he said as he rushed by.

"It's hot in here," Aunt Molly said. She took off her sweater, folded it, and opened the smallest of the three suitcases. She was about to put her sweater into it.

"This isn't mine," Aunt Molly said. She took a very long pair of yellow pants from the suitcase and held them up. She gave the pants to Mrs. Jansen. Then Aunt Molly took out a big shirt and said, "Look at the pineapples and racing cars on this shirt. I would never wear it." She gave the shirt to Mrs. Jansen, too.

Aunt Molly looked through the suitcase. "This is strange," she said. "Nothing in here is mine. Someone packed his clothing in my suitcase."

Chapter Three

Cam looked at the name tag on the suit-case. She showed it to Aunt Molly and told her, "No one packed his clothing in your suitcase. You took the wrong one."

Aunt Molly looked at the tag.

"We should bring this suitcase back," Eric said. "Someone is probably looking for it."

"And one of my suitcases is missing," Aunt Molly said. She took her sweater and walked quickly ahead.

Cam, Eric, and Mr. Jansen followed her.

Mr. Jansen carried Aunt Molly's two large suitcases.

Mrs. Jansen quickly folded the yellow pants and the pineapple shirt and put them into the small suitcase. She closed it and took it with her as she ran to catch up with the others.

Aunt Molly was stopped at the entrance to the luggage area. "I'm sorry, you can't go in there," the guard told her. "It's for passengers only."

"But I am a passenger. I was on Flight 54. My suitcase is still in there."

An older couple was standing near the guard. The woman was wearing a bright red dress. The man was fat and had a short white beard. "And our niece is in there," the woman said. "We have to find her. She just came from France and she doesn't speak any English."

Just then a very tall young man came from the luggage area. "Have you seen anyone leave here with a small brown suitcase?" he asked the guard.

"Is this yours?" Mrs. Jansen asked and showed him the suitcase.

"How did you get that?" the man said. He took the suitcase from Mrs. Jansen.

Aunt Molly leaned close to him and whispered, "That pineapple shirt is ugly. If you put it on, wear a jacket over it."

"Humph," the man said as he walked away.

"I must find my niece," the woman in the red dress said.

The man with her showed the guard a photograph. "This is Simone," he said. "Have you seen her?"

The guard looked at the photograph. He shook his head and said, "I'm sorry, I haven't seen her. But if you wait, I'll have someone look to see if she's inside. And I'll have someone look for your suitcase."

He called over a woman guard with long

curly hair. He told her about Aunt Molly's missing suitcase and showed her the picture of Simone. The guard looked at the photograph and then went inside to look for Simone and the suitcase.

When the guard gave the photograph back to the man, Aunt Molly took a quick look at it.

"I saw Simone," Aunt Molly said. "I saw her on the plane. She sat right across from me. She is very polite. Every time the flight attendant gave her something, she said *merci*. That's French for 'Thank you.' But she didn't eat her applesauce."

Aunt Molly thought for a moment. She was holding her sweater. She brushed some lint off it. Then she said, "She was just ahead of me when I got off the plane. And I think I remember seeing Simone waiting for her luggage."

The woman in the red dress held her hands together, looked up at the ceiling and said, "Oh, I'm so glad she arrived here safely. She's just ten and we were worried."

Cam said, "I'm ten and so is Eric."

"But where is Simone?" the man wanted to know. "She's visiting us for two weeks and we're responsible for her."

"Don't worry," Mrs. Jansen told the woman. "They'll find Simone."

Aunt Molly ate some more popcorn while she waited for the guard to return. Mrs. Jansen tapped on her handbag. And the man told everyone about Simone.

"This is her first trip to visit us. We plan to take her to museums and to the park. We prepared all her favorite foods."

"I hope you didn't make applesauce for her. She doesn't eat it," Aunt Molly said. Then she asked Eric for some more popcorn.

"Here," Eric said and gave her the bag. "You can have what's left."

The woman in the red dress sat on a bench nearby. She leaned forward and said, "If Simone is lost, I don't know what I'll do."

Just then the guard with the long curly hair came out. She told the other guard, "All the luggage is off Flight 54 and it's all been claimed. And I didn't see that girl."

Chapter Four

"Oh, no," the woman in the red dress said. "Simone is missing."

"I hope the gifts I bought are not in that lost suitcase," Aunt Molly said. "I bought a bookmark in the shape of the Eiffel Tower and a toy soldier made of old candy wrappers."

"What should we do now?" Mrs. Jansen asked the guard.

"Go to the airline's service desk. Someone there will help you."

The old man helped his wife off the

bench. Mr. and Mrs. Jansen each carried one of Aunt Molly's suitcases. They followed Cam, Eric, and Aunt Molly to the service desk.

People nearby were sitting on benches and reading newspapers and magazines. Others had their legs stretched out and were resting. There were people rushing past with luggage and people talking to each other. And there were anouncements.

"My name is Charles Green," the old man told the woman behind the airline's desk. "This is my wife Ida. We came to pick up our niece and we can't find her. Her name is Simone Green and she doesn't speak any English."

A tag was pinned to the woman's jacket. "Jill Waner" was printed on the tag.

"Was she on one of our flights?" Jill Waner asked.

"Yes. Flight 54."

Jill Waner picked up the telephone. "First

22

I'll check if she was on the flight."

"Oh, she was on it," Aunt Molly said. "She sat right across from me. She's very polite."

Cam whispered to Eric, "I hope she doesn't tell her about the applesauce."

Jill Waner put the telephone down. "Did you check the luggage area?" she asked.

"Yes."

Jill Waner picked up the phone again. "We'll have her paged. If she's anywhere in the building, she'll hear it."

She spoke to someone over the telephone. Then she told the Greens, "Just wait a few minutes. I'm sure your niece will be here."

"While we wait, maybe you can help me," Aunt Molly said. "I was also on Flight 54 and one of my suitcases is missing."

Jill Waner took two sheets of paper from her desk. "You'll have to fill out these forms," she said. She gave Aunt Molly a pen.

Aunt Molly gave Cam her sweater. Then Aunt Molly sat on a bench. She put the popcorn bag on the bench next to her and began to fill out the forms.

"Jack, they want my local address. That's your house. And they want your telephone number. I always get things with numbers confused. Can you help me with this?"

Mr. Jansen sat on the bench next to Aunt Molly. He began to fill out the forms.

Mrs. Jansen was tapping on her handbag again. She looked at her watch and began tapping her foot on the floor. Then she looked at Cam. "It's silly for you to carry that sweater," she said. "Why don't you put it in Molly's suitcase?"

As Cam opened the suitcase, Mr. Jansen was reading from the form. "Can you describe the lost piece of luggage?" he asked Aunt Molly.

"It's made of canvas. It's small and brown," Aunt Molly said.

"And it has red, yellow, and blue stripes," Cam said.

Aunt Molly and Mr. Jansen turned and saw Cam take a small suitcase out from the larger one.

"Oh, my goodness," Aunt Molly said and laughed. "Now I remember. When I left on my trip my small suitcase was filled with gifts for the friends I would be visiting. When I came back I didn't need it, so I packed it inside one of the bigger suitcases."

"You have your suitcase. Now we can go home," Mrs. Jansen said.

May I have your attention, please, was announced. *Will Simone Green please report to the information desk on the main level. Thank you.*

"That announcement is no good," Cam said. "Simone won't understand it. It should have been made in French."

Mr. Jansen returned the pen and forms to the airline's desk. Then Cam, her parents, Eric, and Aunt Molly began to walk toward the exit.

"Wait," Aunt Molly said. "I forgot something."

"What now?" Mrs. Jansen asked as Aunt Molly ran back to the bench.

A moment later Aunt Molly returned carrying Eric's bag of popcorn. She took some from the bag and ate it as she walked.

"Wait," Eric said.

"Not again," Mrs. Jansen told him. "We have to get home."

"But I know where to find Simone."

Chapter Five

Mr. and Mrs. Jansen put down the suitcases they were carrying. Mrs. Jansen looked at her watch and began tapping her fingers on her handbag again. Aunt Molly took some more popcorn from the bag.

"You're hungry, right?" Eric asked Aunt Molly.

"Yes, I never get enough to eat on an airplane."

"Well, if you're hungry, Simone must be hungry, too. She's probably in one of the restaurants eating."

Cam, Eric, and Aunt Molly rushed over to the Greens. "We know where to find Simone," Eric told them.

"Aunt Molly just got off the same flight and she's real hungry," Cam said.

"And I even brought along something to eat on the airplane. I had a buttered roll in my handbag," Aunt Molly said.

"We think Simone must be hungry, too. We'll probably find her in one of the restaurants."

Charles Green said, "You may be right. Let's go and look."

"No, we have to stay right here," Ida Green said. "I've asked them to repeat the announcement, this time in French. I hope Simone hears it. And if she does, I want to be here to meet her."

"We have to go home now," Mrs. Jansen told Cam, Eric, and Aunt Molly. Then she said to the Greens, "I'm sure you'll find Simone."

"We can't leave now," Cam told her mother.

Mrs. Jansen whispered, "But I have to get home. You know that. And you know why."

"What's that? Why do you have to get home?" Aunt Molly asked.

"Oh, I have some things to do," Mrs. Jansen said.

"We don't live far from the airport. I'll take you home now," Mr. Jansen told his wife. "Then I'll come back and pick up Molly, Cam, and Eric."

"And while you're gone, we'll find Simone," Eric said.

Mr. Jansen looked at his watch. "I'll be back at 3:00. I'll be at the main entrance."

Mr. and Mrs. Jansen walked toward the exit. Mr. Green showed the photograph of Simone to Cam and Eric. Cam looked at it, blinked her eyes and said, *"Click."*

Eric explained to Mr. Green, "That *click* helps Cam to remember the picture."

"Oh."

Aunt Molly looked at the photograph again. "Simone's hair is longer now. She has it in a ponytail. And she's wearing a blue shirt."

Aunt Molly returned the photograph to Mr. Green. Cam, Eric, and Aunt Molly started to walk to one of the restaurants. Mr. Jansen ran to them. He took a deep breath and then said, "Molly, I wanted to make sure you knew that we have your suitcases."

"Oh no, I've lost them again."

"No, you haven't lost them. I have your suitcases in the car. I'm taking them home."

"Good," Cam said. "Now let's find Simone."

Cam, Eric, and Aunt Molly went first to a small coffee shop on the main level. A few people were sitting by the counter and eating. Simone was not there.

They went next to a fancy restaurant. Soft music was playing and there was very little light. A man wearing a bow tie and a black suit greeted them.

"Would you like to be seated?" the man asked Aunt Molly.

"No. We're looking for someone."

Cam, Eric, and Aunt Molly walked quietly
through the restaurant. The man followed
them. "Please," he whispered. "Don't disturb
anyone."

"But there's no one here. This place is
empty," Cam said.

May I have your attention please, Cam, Eric, and Aunt Molly heard as they left the restaurant. *Will Simone Green please report to the information desk. Thank you.* Then the announcement was repeated in French. *Simone Green, est priée de se presenter à l'information. Merci.*

Cam, Eric, and Aunt Molly walked past the information desk. They saw the Greens sitting nearby. They waited a short while. When Simone didn't come, they walked toward the escalator.

Eric said, "She's probably eating downstairs. Maybe she doesn't know where the information desk is and everyone she asks doesn't speak French."

Just as Cam, Eric, and Aunt Molly got on the "down" escalator, a few people got off the "up" escalator.

"Did you see her? Did you see who just got off?" Cam asked.

"I saw a skinny woman with sunglasses

and a few cameras," Aunt Molly said.

"I saw a woman wearing lots of colored beads," Eric said.

"No," Cam said as the escalator took them downstairs. "I saw a girl with a ponytail. I saw Simone."

Chapter Six

Eric turned and started to walk up the "down" escalator. People moved aside to let him pass. But as Eric walked up, the escalator kept going down.

Cam and Aunt Molly got off the escalator on the lower level. They turned and got on the "up" escalator. Eric was still near the bottom of the "down" escalator. He turned and got off.

"Wait for me," Eric called to Cam and Aunt Molly. "I'll be up in a minute."

When Cam and Aunt Molly reached the

main level, they looked for the girl with the ponytail. Cam said, "I'm not sure which way she went."

"Here I am," Eric said.

"I'll walk this way to look for Simone," Cam said and pointed to her left. Then she pointed to her right and told Eric, "You look this way."

"And I'll walk straight ahead," Aunt Molly said.

Cam walked quickly to her left. There were many small groups of people. Two women were hugging. One of them kept saying, "It's so good to see you."

Cam passed a man who was telling a few people, "I rode on a camel. Can you believe that! And I went on a boat with a glass bottom and saw thousands of fish."

Cam looked at all the people. Then she saw the girl with the ponytail. Cam ran to her.

"Simone, Simone," Cam said.

The girl looked at Cam.

"French. *Merci*. Simone," Cam said.

The girl shook her head. "French, mercy, see, moan? What are you talking about?"

"Then you're not Simone Green. You're not lost."

"Of course not," the girl said and walked away.

Cam walked to meet Eric and Aunt Molly. "I found the girl with the ponytail," Cam told them, "but she wasn't Simone."

39

Aunt Molly looked at her watch. "It's almost 3:00. We'll have to go to the main entrance to meet your father," she said.

As Cam, Eric, and Aunt Molly walked toward the entrance, they passed the Greens. Eric told them, "I'm sorry. But we didn't find Simone."

Mrs. Green was sitting on a bench. She looked up for a moment. When she didn't see Simone, she looked down again.

"Ida is very upset," Mr. Green told Cam, Eric, and Aunt Molly. "We were both hoping you would find Simone. But thank you so much for your help."

"Look, there's your father," Aunt Molly said as she waved to Mr. Jansen.

"We have to go now," Eric told Mr. Green.

Cam, Eric, and Aunt Molly were walking toward Mr. Jansen when, *May I have your attention please,* was announced. *The city bus will be leaving in three minutes. Thank you.*

Three women pulling suitcases on wheels

rushed past. Then came a tall man with a small boy walking beside him. The man was taking quick, long steps. The small boy had to run to keep up with him. "Hurry, or we'll miss the bus," the man said.

Cam looked at the tall man. Then she closed her eyes and said, "*Click.*"

Aunt Molly heard Cam say "*Click.*" She saw that Cam's eyes were closed. Aunt Molly held Cam's hand and walked with her to Mr. Jansen.

Cam opened her eyes and said, "Hi, Dad." Then she closed her eyes again and said, "*Click*."

We didn't find Simone," Eric whispered. "But now Cam is using her mental camera. Maybe she'll remember an important clue."

Cam's eyes were still closed. Her father held one of her hands. Aunt Molly held the other. They walked with Cam to the car. Eric followed them.

"*Click*," Cam said as they were crossing the street. "*Click*," she said again as she got into the car.

Cam opened her eyes just as her father was driving out of the airport parking lot. "Don't go this way. Follow the bus to the city," Cam said.

"What?"

"Follow the bus to the city. I think we'll find Simone standing at one of the bus stops."

Chapter Seven

Mr. Jansen drove the car to the side of the road. He turned off the car's engine and then turned and looked at Cam.

"Why do you think you'll find Simone at one of the bus stops?"

"The Greens don't know what Simone looks like, so they have a picture of her. And I'm sure that Simone has a picture of the Greens. If she saw someone who looked like the picture, she would follow him."

"But why do you think Simone is at one of the bus stops?" Cam's father asked again.

"Just when Aunt Molly was coming out with her luggage there was an announcement for the city bus. One of the people rushing for the bus was an old, fat man with a white beard. He bumped into Eric. Mr. Green is fat. He's old and he has a white beard. I think Simone might have followed that man. She may have thought he was her uncle."

Mr. Jansen started the car and said, "We'll follow the bus for a few stops, but I don't think we'll find Simone."

Mr. Jansen drove on. He found the bus waiting at one of the traffic lights. It was a blue bus with a red roof. When the traffic light changed to green, and the bus moved ahead, Mr. Jansen followed it.

Eric asked Cam, "But wouldn't the man have told Simone that he was not her uncle?"

"The man was in a hurry. He probably didn't even know Simone was following him until he got on the bus. And if he doesn't speak French it may have taken a while for him to realize what Simone wanted."

The bus stopped. Mr. Jansen stopped his car, too. Cam and Eric looked at the people waiting on both sides of the street. They didn't see Simone.

A few people got off the bus. Then it drove away from the stop and Mr. Jansen followed it.

"I saw lots of castles on this trip," Aunt Molly said. "I even went into two of them. They were real cold and drafty inside. Kings and queens must have lots of sweaters."

The bus stopped again. The three women with suitcases on wheels got off. The bus doors closed and the bus drove away. Mr. Jansen was about to follow it.

"Stop, Dad. I see her. She's across the street," Cam said.

Cam and Eric got out of the car. They walked to the corner and waited for the traffic light to change to green. Then they crossed the street.

"Hi, Simone. I'm Cam."

"And my name is Eric."

"*Que?*"

"My name is Eric," he said again, louder and very slowly.

"*Je ne comprends pas.*"

"Simone, look at this," Cam said. She stretched out her arms, flapped them, and made airplane noises.

"*Brrrr. Brrrr. Brum, brum, brum.*"

Then Cam took a few small steps and

46

moved her head all around as if she was looking for someone.

"*Qu'avez-vous?*"

Eric pointed to Simone and said, "Simone Green?"

"*Oui.*"

"I think '*we*' means 'yes.'" Eric said to Cam.

Eric pointed in the direction of the airport and said, "Charles and Ida Green."

"*Oui.*"

"Come with us," Cam said to Simone. But as she and Eric walked toward the car, Simone didn't follow them.

"We're strangers to her," Eric said. "She won't go in the car with us."

Aunt Molly had crossed the street. She said that she would wait with Simone. Cam and Eric would return to the airport and get the Greens.

"I'm glad you found Simone," Mr. Jansen told Cam and Eric while they were on their way to the airport. "But we have to hurry. By now there's a crowd of people waiting at home to surprise Molly."

The Greens were happy to see Cam and Eric again. And when they told the Greens that they had found Simone, Mrs. Green hugged Cam and Eric.

The Greens had called the airport guards

and the police and asked them to look for Simone. Now they called again and told them that Simone was found. Then they went in Mr. Jansen's car.

"You thought that Simone might be hungry," Mr. Green said to Eric in the car. "So while we were waiting, I bought her a few things to eat."

Mr. Green took a wrapped egg salad sandwich from one pocket. He took some packaged cookies and dried fruit from another pocket. "And Ida has a can of juice in her handbag."

"There she is. I see her," Mrs. Green said.

Mr. Jansen stopped the car. The Greens got out, crossed the street, and ran to Simone.

"They're all so happy," Aunt Molly said when she opened the car door and got inside.

A moment later Mr. and Mrs. Green came to the car. They were each carrying one of

Simone's suitcases. Mrs. Green was holding Simone's hand

"Can I drive you someplace?" Mr. Jansen asked.

"No. We'll take the bus," Mr. Green said. "We want to thank you again for finding Simone."

"*Merci. Merci,*" Simone said. She smiled and waved as Mr. Jansen drove away.

Chapter Eight

"Jennifer, I'm proud of you. And I'm proud of you, too, Eric," Mr. Jansen said as he drove.

"That was exciting," Aunt Molly said. "As soon as Cam closed her eyes and said, '*Cluck*' I knew she would find Simone."

Eric laughed. "Chickens say '*Cluck*.' Cam says '*Click*,' like a camera."

"There were chickens on the road to one of the castles I visited. The driver stopped the tour bus a few times to let them go past."

Mr. Jansen parked the car in front of their

house. "Oh my, look how pretty your garden is," Aunt Molly said as she opened the car door.

Cam and Eric quickly got out of the car. "We'll go and tell Mom that you're coming," Cam said as they ran to the house.

Cam and Eric opened the door. People were standing in the living room and talking.

"She's coming," Cam told them.

Two women quickly hid behind the living

room curtains. A few people hid behind the couch and chairs. Eric's father and mother took the baby and hid in the dining room. Eric's twin sisters, Donna and Diane, hid in the kitchen.

Aunt Molly walked into the house. She looked around.

"Surprise!" Eric's parents and the others called as they came out of hiding. Mrs. Jansen came in carrying a large cake. "Happy Birthday Molly," was written on the cake.

"But my birthday is April 7," Aunt Molly said.

"That's today," Mr. Jansen told her.

Aunt Molly greeted her friends. "And this must be little Harry," she said when she saw Eric's baby brother.

"He's Howie," Eric told her.

"And you must be Darlene and Dora," she said when she saw Eric's sisters.

"No, I'm Donna."

"And I'm Diane."

Aunt Molly looked at all her friends. "Oh, I'm so happy," she said. "I need a handkerchief. I think I'm going to cry."

Aunt Molly opened her handbag. "What's this?" She took out something covered with foil. She unwrapped a buttered roll.

"That's why I was so hungry. I never ate my roll," Aunt Molly said.

"Don't eat that roll. I have fresh sandwiches, salads, and cake for you to eat," Mrs. Jansen said.

"But first we should sing 'Happy Birthday,'" Cam said.

"Sure. Let's sing," Aunt Molly said. "Whose birthday is it?"

Everyone looked at Aunt Molly. She smiled. Then she laughed. "Oh, I know it's my birthday. It says so on the cake."

Everyone laughed and sang "Happy Birthday" to Aunt Molly. Aunt Molly sang, too.